Jerry's Magic

W.W. Rowe

LARSON PUBLICATIONS
BURDETT, NEW YORK

Copyright © 2014 by W.W. Rowe

ISBN-10: 1-936012-66-9
ISBN-13: 978-1-936012-66-4
Library of Congress Control Number: 2014936521

Publisher's Cataloging-In-Publication Data
(Prepared by The Donohue Group, Inc.)

Rowe, William Woodin.
  Jerry's magic / W.W. Rowe.

    pages : illustrations ; cm

    Summary: Ten-year old Jerry Shore is the man of the house and makes good
money selling and renting magical objects he gets from the Wonderworker
by the dump. When some of the objects don't work, kids at school demand
their money back. However, Jerry has already spent it and would be in big
trouble if not for The Doubler, which doubles money left in it overnight.
The Wonderworker cautions him not to misuse The Doubler and helps him
discover his higher self.
    Interest age level: 008-012.
    Issued also as an ebook.
    ISBN-13: 978-1-936012-66-4
    ISBN-10: 1-936012-66-9

    1. Boys--Conduct of life--Juvenile fiction. 2. Magic--Juvenile fiction.
3. Money--Juvenile fiction. 4. Boys--Conduct of life--Fiction. 5. Magic--
Fiction. 6. Money--Fiction. I. Title.

PZ7.R7953 Je 2014
[Fic]   2014936521

Published by Larson Publications
4936 NYS Route 414
Burdett, New York 14818 USA

larsonpublications.com

24 23 22 21 20 19 18 17 16 15 14

10 9 8 7 6 5 4 3 2 1

Inspiration and Influence
(the Prince and the Pauper)
are tricky twins.

This book is gratefully dedicated to
Mark Twain, Paul Brunton, and
my wife Eleanor.

The annals of hypnotism amply prove this
possibility of making an external world exist
before our eyes even though it is a form of
consciousness and nothing more.
—Paul Brunton, *The Wisdom of the Overself*

I have met people who could hypnotize you to do
anything they want and you don't know it.
—Anthony Damiani, *Looking Into Mind*

It was, I believe, Matthew Arnold who first
used this term "higher self," and it is certainly
expressive enough for our present purpose.
—Paul Brunton, *Inspiration and the Overself*

On Magic

DO you believe in magic? Not *ordinary* magic. Not when a man with a sneaky smile pours water into his hat, and then pours it out as confetti. Or when he pulls, from that same hat, a terrified, kicking rabbit.

No, I mean *real* magic. When something unbelievable happens. Something that changes your life in deep, amazing ways you might never have thought possible. That's what this book is really about.

Do you know someone very old? Someone who lived before smart phones, the Internet, or even TV? A person who has magical stories to tell about a childhood in a different world? This book is about that too.

So pull up your eyes and start reading! If you discover some magic, please don't brag. But it's okay to recommend this awesome book to everyone you know.

Disclaimer

IF you start doing some amazing things after you read this book, the author assumes no responsibility. Ditto if you acquire any magic powers. If you learn how to make gobs of money from this story (or from any of Jerry's adventures that follow), it is probably a coincidence. And if you learn how to awesomely influence your friends, please do not blame it on this book. Just be kind to those unsuspecting friends.

ONE

JARED SHORE has tangled, sandy hair and big, brown eyes. He's ten, going on a hundred and ten. At least, that's what his mama says.

"That boy is scare-your-socks-off smart," she declares to anyone who will listen. "Just last week, Jerry taught his pet snake to dance. Dance, mind you! And he never got bit even once. But I felt kinda relieved when Slippy sneaked off into the woods."

His mama goes on and on, telling about how Jerry foiled two bank-robbers singlehanded. How he sold an old, broken hand mirror to a pushy man who came to the front door selling brushes. How he said the mirror was a Future Scope that could show glimpses of what was to come, including the first alien creatures to invade this planet. And how he secretly gobbled down five entire chocolate cakes at the church picnic. Then she makes a sweet, perfect smile with her false teeth, hardly noticing that her listeners are backing away, rolling their eyes like she's totally loony.

So what if the five chocolate cakes were cupcakes? So what if the snake "danced" by raising its head and swaying from side to side? Truth can be hard to get ahold of, like Slippy slithering away into the woods. But you can always know your own truth, deep down inside your heart.

Jerry's papa died fighting in the big war in 1942 when the boy was five, and his mama is still reeling from her grief. Some mornings, she sprinkles sugar on Jerry's scrambled eggs instead of salt! Once she poured orange juice into her own coffee—and gave birdseed to Jade, the cat. She even wore her husband's necktie to church, like a striped blue belt around her waist.

Jerry laughs at his mama's silliness, but he broke a finger hitting the wall of his room. Even after that, he punched his pillow at night for several months. In bed, the warm tears, running down the sides of his face, turned cold when they reached his ears. Staring up into the darkness, he could almost see his papa's floating, smiling face.

After receiving the terrible news, Jerry's mama stopped weeping long enough to say, "You're the man of the mansion now, honey." Then she chuckled grimly, because their old house was so small and dilapidated.

She might have thought Jerry didn't understand, but he did. Oh, yes, he did! The man of the mansion brought in money. Fistfuls of money. And that very day, Jerry resolved to be a big moneymaker.

He began by selling his old toys for high prices to his worst friends, the ones he didn't mind swindling. The boy, it soon developed, had a golden, persuasive tongue. The cash he received was pure profit, but he spent it all on candy bars and strawberry sodas.

When Jerry was seven, he sneaked into the local bank to learn more about money. Checks were the answer. If you had a check, they'd give you piles of money! But when he asked his mama where he could buy some checks, she cackled until she had a choking fit.

One day, when Jerry was about to ask a lady at the bank how he could get a few checks, two tough-looking men came rushing in. They held out long, scary guns. "Freeze!" they shouted. "Down on the floor, and nobody gets hurt."

Some people panicked, gasping and screaming. Others dropped obediently to the floor, only to get tripped over. One man actually peed in his pants. One lady fainted dead away. Then the screaming and shrieking grew even louder. "Quiet!" one of the men yelled. "Or we start shooting."

During the commotion, Jerry slid beneath one of the teller's gates to hide. He didn't want to get shot! The teller wasn't there, but as Jerry crawled behind the counter wall, his hand pressed down on a little bump in the rug.

Instantly, a loud, clanging alarm rang out. The robbers snarled angrily. After a brief huddle, they turned and fled . . . right into the arms of four policemen! Fortunately, they had been driving by and heard the alarm.

Before long, one of the policemen was shaking Jerry's hand. "Quick thinking, son," he told him. But when Jerry asked for a reward, the policeman laughed and slapped him on the back. "No flies on you, boy!" he chortled.

So that was how Jerry, in his mama's words, foiled two bank-robbers singlehanded.

TWO

NOW that's he's ten, Jerry gets ten cents a week for doing chores and a nickel to put in the collection plate on Sunday. A dime buys two Hershey bars, two Pepsis, or two Cokes. Comic books are ten cents, and he loves Plastic Man. If you look for Plastic Man's red and yellow colors, you can often spot him disguised as a chair or even a big vase before he appears as himself.

Jerry makes good money now. How? By dealing in valuable objects. Magical objects! Every once in a while, he mysteriously acquires a new one. And there are rumors, cleverly started by Jerry himself, that he possesses weird magical powers. If he feels like it, he can give you bad luck for a week. Or headaches and even a green rash.

Jerry has a shimmery, rainbow-colored mist around him. It's called a mystical aura, and it's visible only to someone with similar powers. And he's learning to "cloud your mind," like The Shadow, so you can't see him at all! Some of the kids in Jerry's school shiver at such thoughts. Others laugh and scoff, but only when he's too far away to hear them.

Jerry owns a clear, shiny object that resembles an empty glass jar for preserves. But it's really a Bad-Dream Protector. It keeps nightmares away for sure, unless they're sent by an evil Wizard, and there's no earthly way to stop those. If you're having a spell of bad dreams, you can rent The Protector from Jerry for fifty cents a night.

Jerry also has a cool thing called an Enchanted Viewer. It looks like an empty cardboard toilet paper roll, but appearances can be deceiving. Hold The Viewer up against the wall, and you can see right through it! You can only see a little circle of what's on the other side, but it's still amazing. You don't get to see through solid matter every day.

Jerry is accepting money for peeks into the girls' locker room at the gym. For only a dollar, he'll let you use The Viewer, as soon as it's ready. The thing is, its powers are "temperamental," and it hasn't quite "activated" yet. But the money keeps rolling in.

Some of the guys are getting impatient for a look through The Viewer. One day, Cromer Borkin, a clumsy bull of a boy, corners Jerry. "I paid you two weeks ago," he says, wheezing through his fat nose. "Let's have some action!" Cromer is very strong. His hobby is pushing down old dead trees in the forest. Then he thumps his chest and roars with laughter.

Willie Fielder, a sly, sneaky boy who sits next to

Jerry and copies his answers on tests, grabs Cromer's arm. "Careful," he whispers. "Remember the green rash. The bad luck, too. You don't need to mess with them things."

Cromer shrugs off Willie's hand. "That's a bunch of bull," he growls. "You ever seen a green rash? I wanna look through The Viewer now!"

Jerry gives Cromer a cold, powerful look. "You can't rush magic," he smoothly declares, though he feels pretty quaky inside. "The Viewer is temporarily discombobulated. Once I tried to hurry my Future Scope, and it stopped working altogether. I had to get rid of it."

* * *

Two days later, Peter Wardly comes to school with fire in his eyes. He's a tall boy with a face like a dignified rat. Peter marches right up to Jerry and demands his buck-fifty back. "I paid you for three nights," he complains, holding up The Bad-Dream Protector. "And last night I dreamed of a slimy monster with razor-sharp teeth. It ate off both my legs before I woke up." Peter stamps his newly restored foot. "Stick this gyp up your butt and gimme back my money!"

By this time, a crowd of curious kids has gathered. Evidently, Peter is willing to brave the headaches, the bad luck, and the green rash. The kids all stand in a gaping ring around Peter and Jerry.

Some of the girls are growing suspicious. Their good-luck rusty-nail charms might be fakes too! Eva Ning softly hisses at Jerry. Molly Kewel sneers. They finger the charms that hang on loops of string around their necks.

But Suzie Steele watches anxiously. She's a pretty girl with springy golden curls, and Jerry's sweet on her. She likes him too, and now, her dark eyes are frightened and wide. She tightly squeezes the charm around her neck. She believes it's definitely real.

"Well?" says rat-faced Peter—and a hush falls over the crowd. It's so quiet, you can hear Peter's teeth grinding. Suzie holds her breath.

Jerry stares Peter powerfully, coldly in the eye, even though he's feeling panicky inside. "Did you say the secret words?"

"What secret words?" says Peter. His lip curls into a defiant snarl. Fortunately, he's not very bright.

"The secret words I told you, of course." Jerry looks shocked. "Don't tell me you forgot!" Now he looks painfully disappointed. "Those words activate the magic. Don't you remember?"

Peter hesitates. He's racking his brains, but can't remember any secret words at all. Just yesterday, he couldn't say when the War of 1812 took place! True, he was daydreaming when the teacher called on him, but he doesn't want to seem stupid again. "I . . . I might've forgot the secret words just that once. Yes, I guess that's what happened."

Jerry heaves a sigh of relief, which he quickly passes off as exasperation. "Oh well, then. If you don't use

The Protector correctly, you can't expect it to work." He hands the shiny glass object back to Peter. "Keep it beside your bed for three more nights, but remember to say the secret words. I'll even let you wait to pay me another buck-fifty until after you use it."

Peter takes The Protector back, mumbling something like "Thanks." The crowd breaks up. It's time for class.

This gives Jerry time to think up some powerful-sounding words. Which is good, because later, on the playing field, Peter sheepishly asks him to say the secret words again, to be sure he's got them exactly right.

Jerry sighs. He tells Peter his brain needs cleaning out with a long pipe cleaner. Cromer, who overhears this, laughs and slaps his thigh. Then Jerry whispers two outlandish tongue twisters in Peter's ear.

Three days later, Peter gives Jerry two one-dollar bills and four quarters. "This is for the last three nights, and the next three too," he tells him. "The Protector is working fine now with the, uh, secret words."

*　　*　　*

That night at supper, Jerry's mama plinks down her teacup. "What happened at school today, dear?"

Jerry licks his empty ice cream spoon. "Uh, nothing, Mama."

"That's funny. You look a little worried." She lifts the cup to her lips and studies him over it.

"School can be tough, Mama."

"But you're getting good grades, dear. Mr. Filkins says—"

"It's not the teachers." Jerry frowns. "Some of the guys."

"Want to talk about it?"

"No."

Jerry's mama shudders, her lips moving silently. "Have courage, dear. You have *royal blood* in you. That will give you strength to carry on."

"I know, Mama. The Duke of Derring-Do."

His mama solemnly nods. "But not only that, honey. You're a direct descendant of Sir Stalwart, Earl of Intrepid. So take heart."

Jerry smiles weakly. "I know that too, Mama."

She sighs. "Well, I've had my own troubles. I had to ring for Bodkins three times before he deigned to come to the library. Some of our rare books desperately needed dusting. The leather-bound editions of Shakespeare, Dickens, Mark Twain, Matthew Arnold . . . I swear I don't know what that butler does, all alone in his room."

Jerry smiles. "Maybe he's building a bomb, Mama."

"Mercy! I hope not. We don't need to have a blast, hee hee." She seems pleased her little joke. "Well, when you finish, put your finger bowl in the sink. Clara will wash it."

THREE

TIME marches by, like a parade of impatient soldiers. The guys who paid to use The Viewer are getting real antsy.

"When is that thing gonna activate?" Cromer Borkin demands. "It's taking forever!"

"Yeah," says Willie Fielder, who paid an extra dollar just to go first. "You rippin' us off, or what?"

Jerry backs up a little. "I'll see if I can hurry it," he tells them. "But it's very temperamental."

Deep inside, Jerry knows he's headed for trouble. Big trouble. He's already spent most of the money on comic books, Fleer's "Double Bubble" gum (you can get it now, after the war!), and strawberry sodas. And to be completely honest—something he tries to avoid— he isn't really sure if the "temperamental" Viewer will ever work.

But Jerry has an ace up his sleeve: Crazy Wilcox. The man some people laugh at when they ought to be more careful. The man who lives in a cardboard house at the edge of the junkyard. The man who became Jerry's friend after his papa died. The man who gives Jerry his magical objects, including the Future Scope before it stopped working altogether.

So on Saturday morning, making sure he's not being followed, Jerry heads for the junkyard. Crazy Wilcox will probably be home because he almost never goes out. He can sit in one place almost forever!

Sure enough, the bearded old man is sitting cross-legged in front of his house. He's wearing jeans, a dark-blue sweater, and a faded red headband. His eyes are totally closed, but when Jerry gets near, he uncannily raises one hand. "Greetings, young friend!" He opens his eyes and smiles. "What brings you to the Wonderworker?"

Jerry blinks. He didn't even know Crazy Wilcox was called that! But you can never tell about magic people. Surprises are part of their magic. "Hi, uh, Wonderworker," he says. "I need your help. I'm in a bad predicament."

The man's smile vanishes. He quickly removes his red headband and passes it through his fingers. Suddenly, it's bright green!

Jerry gapes, even though he's seen this trick before. At least, he's seen the headband turn yellow. Also orange. Blue too.

Now, the Wonderworker gives the headband a swirling shake, and it suddenly returns to its faded red color. He ties it smoothly around his head. "What kind of predicament, Turnip?"

Turnip! Another surprise. He's been Puppy and Big Guy and Pal, but never Turnip. Jerry laughs in spite of his troubles. Crazy Wilcox has a way of making you feel better even without doing any magic. "I need to get The Viewer working. Lots of guys paid me to use it."

The Wonderworker raises his eyebrows. "Really? Sit down for a spell." He pats the ground beside him. "The magic headband just whispered in my ear that you've spent all the money. Is that right?"

"Uh, yeah. Nearly all, anyway. I can't pay it back, either."

Wilcox frowns darkly. "Not good, Turnip. Not good at all." He clucks his tongue. "Not good to borrow and be broke tomorrow. You did borrow the money, didn't you? You didn't *intend* to keep it if The Viewer failed to work?"

Jerry squirms. He tries to be honest. "I think so. I mean . . . I'm not really sure. The money just got spent. I love strawberry sodas. But if I could just make The Viewer work, then maybe . . ." His words trail away, like dogs wandering off into a cornfield.

The Wonderworker nods. "Keep your intentions pure, Turnip. Let your Higher Self take over."

"My what?"

"Your Higher Self. Everybody has one. It's the best part of you, the part closest to God. It's indestructible and immortal. In some ways, it's like a guardian angel. It helps you to do . . . what is honest and true." Wilcox smiles. "It's fine to make some dough. Not if you're shady, though." He closes his eyes, like he's deep in thought.

Jerry sits there beside him, not sure what to do. He can smell rotten orange peels and sour milk drifting over from the junkyard. Not far away, two invisible birds warble back and forth.

"Bwa-ha!" The old man's eyes fly open. "My headband just whispered the answer. You need a Money-Doubler."

"A what?"

"That's right." The Wonderworker is bending over a pile of trash. "A Money-Doubler. And I just stumbled on one!" Snatching up what looks like an old cigar box, he flips it open. His eyes are burning like twin fires. "How much cash do you have, Turnip?"

Jerry thinks for a minute. "Seventy-five cents in my pocket. Two-fifty in my blue soldier bank. And a quarter on my desk. To flip for difficult homework questions."

The old man smiles. "That's three-fifty. How much will you owe if The Viewer doesn't work?"

Jerry's face reddens. "Twenty-five, maybe twenty-eight dollars."

"Perfect!" The Wonderworker grins broadly. He makes some magic passes through the air with his hands. "Three-fifty doubled is seven. Once more makes fourteen. Then twenty-eight. Use The Doubler three times and bring it back to me." He holds out the box, smoothly flipping it shut. "Remember to be sure . . . your intentions are pure."

Jerry's heart leaps. "Thanks! But, uh, how do I use The Doubler?"

FOUR

THE WONDERWORKER lowers his voice. "That big pine tree behind your house," he says. "Put all your money in The Doubler—neatly, so it understands that you respect it, and what it will do for you. Then leave it under the tree, at midnight."

"Okay," says Jerry. "But how did you know about the pine tree?"

The old man laughs. "The magic headband whispered in my ear. You'd be surprised, all the things it knows. Anyway, leave your money there for three nights in a row."

Jerry gulps. "You mean, let it keep doubling?"

The Wonderworker solemnly nods. "But keep it in your room during the day. Now here's the key. Say this charm every night, when you leave The Doubler under the tree." He puckers up his face and growls out two magic words. It sounds like two bulldogs, arguing over a bone. "Got it?" He stares coldly and deeply into Jerry's eyes, and for a moment, the whole world seems to wobble and spin.

"I . . . think so," says Jerry when his eyes settle down. Wow! When Wilcox gives you The Look, it sure has a powerful effect! And now, Jerry repeats the charm almost perfectly, feeling an amazing vibration on his tongue as he does so.

"Excellent," the Wonderworker declares. "But only use The Doubler for three nights. When you reach twenty-eight dollars, return it to me." He raises a long finger. "Keep this a secret! The Doubler won't work if anyone watches it, including you. If anyone finds out, all your money might disappear. The Doubler might decide to swallow it whole!"

Jerry gasps. "You mean . . . it's alive?"

"Not exactly. But the magic is. Now remember: no more than three times. Don't try to fry your fish in the sky!"

Jerry nods. He thinks he understands, but he's ashamed to ask exactly what it means. "I won't do that," he says. "Thanks, Wonderworker!"

*   *   *

Perhaps you've been wondering why that pushy brush salesman bought the broken hand mirror from Jerry. The one he called a Future Scope. Even with his golden, persuasive tongue, how could Jerry have swindled the man? It was mostly because of The Look that Crazy Wilcox does. That Look, if you do it just right, can make a person do whatever you want!

Wilcox has been teaching The Look to Jerry, but he's still new at it. First he tried it out on Jade the cat, but she only hissed and arched her back. But then he tried it on the brush salesman, and The Look worked perfectly.

The man stuck his foot in the door and talked a blue streak. He showed Jerry's mama a set of hairbrushes trimmed in real gold. Jerry noticed that the gold was peeling off the edge of one brush, but the man quickly covered it with his thumb.

"This is the bargain of a lifetime!" he declared. The man was on the point of making a sale when Jerry jostled his elbow. "Don't interrupt, sonny," he said. "I'm trying to explain to your—"

Jerry was staring up into his eyes, coldly and powerfully. The salesman held onto the wall to keep from falling. "Whoa! Dizzy spell."

"See this object?" said Jerry, holding up the broken mirror. "It's a valuable Future Scope. It has a magic surface. If you gaze into it, long and hard, you can see things that will happen in the future." He puffed his chest out proudly. "My favorite is the first alien creatures to invade this planet. But make sure you're sitting down. It's real scary."

The salesman paid him fifteen dollars and thanked him in the bargain!

But later, when Jerry tried The Look on Cromer, and on Peter, they didn't seem to feel its power at all.

One time he tried it on his mama, because she was getting a little too bossy. But when he looked powerfully, coldly, and deeply into her eyes, she cackled until the tears slid down her cheeks.

FIVE

JERRY gets home with the precious Doubler hidden beneath his shirt. He must look like he's gained twenty pounds. Fortunately (could it be the magical influence of the Wonderworker?) his mama is out, so he rushes up to his room and hides the box deep in his closet.

Now he's doing his homework, but his mind is on his money. Will The Doubler work? He wants to get out of this mess! He wants to let his Higher Self take over, even though he's not sure what that is. Doubling his money will be a good start. He practices growling the charm in his head until he hears the kitchen door slam.

"Jerry! You up there? We're having mac and cheese for supper. Your favorite! And turnips."

Jerry feels prickles all over. Wilcox just called him Turnip! And now he's influenced his mama to buy some, just to prove The Doubler will work. Jerry grins. "Sounds good, Mama!"

"Take a splash in your marble bath, dear. Hee hee! Henri should have dinner ready soon."

"Okay, Mama." Jerry barely hears her. His mind is on The Doubler. It's enough to make you want to learn math. Wilcox had it right: three-fifty, seven, fourteen, twenty-eight . . . But why only three times? That was the question! Still musing about it, he almost stumbles down the stairs.

The mac and cheese is lip-smackin' tasty. Jerry has two huge helpings. Even a few turnips. He's hungry, burning off energy just thinking about what he'll do at midnight.

His mama plinks down her teacup. "What's on your mind, honey?"

"Nothing." Jerry squirms a little (the Wonder-worker's influence?) and quickly adds: "Nothing much."

His mama sniffs suspiciously. "Where did you go today?"

"I took a walk . . . over to the junkyard."

"Did you bring back another magical object?"

Oh, no! The Doubler has to be a secret! Jerry shovels in a heap of mac and cheese, so he can think.

"Did you?"

Jerry swallows slowly. He's sailing on a dangerous, stormy sea! "Yes, but I can't say what it is . . . until it works."

His mama sniffs again, like a bloodhound getting on to something. "Did you see Crazy Wilcox?"

"Uh, yes, Mama. He helped me with a problem . . . about some guys at school." There. He's left the stormy sea for a safe harbor.

"Jerry! I told you to stay away from that man. He's loonier than I am!"

Jerry smiles. "No, he's not, Mama."

"Oh, so you think *I'm* loonier?"

Jerry turns red. "Uh, no, Mama. Not at all." He starts spooning himself a third helping.

"That's enough mac and cheese, dear. I don't want to see it again, like I did those five chocolate cakes."

"They were big cupcakes, Mama. Anyway, I made it to the door."

"Still." She sighs. "Poor Jade was on the porch, and I had to give her a bath. Hissed like a teakettle, she did. At least, you managed to miss the oriental rugs, hee hee."

Jerry pokes the serving spoon back in the mac. He's just had a terrible thought. How can he sneak down past his mama at midnight? Her bedroom's at the foot of the stairs, and she's such a light sleeper! The floors creak, too.

"Mama! Can you see a bug bite on my nose?"

She leans closer, across the rickety kitchen table. "No, honey. Where?"

Jerry stares coldly, powerfully into her eyes.

But she only laughs. "You're looking like you did with that brush salesman. Wasn't that funny? He paid you fifteen dollars for that piece of junk, hee hee! But I don't see any bite."

Jerry gives up on The Look. He's thought of a way out. Climb down the drainpipe. He did it once last summer, and never fell at all.

"You'll need to help with the dishes, dear." His mama sighs. "It's Clara's night off."

"Yes, Mama."

"Oh, and leave your shoes outside your door tonight. Bodkins will touch them up for church tomorrow."

* * *

Jerry's lying on his side, one eye fixed on the luminous clock beside his bed. It takes forever for that pesky minute hand to move! Finally, five minutes of twelve. The time he planned to spring into action. The Doubler, now containing his entire three-fifty, sits on the floor beneath his bed.

The window goes up real quiet. No chance that'll wake her. Now he's sliding carefully down the drainpipe. It's hard with The Doubler under his pajama shirt, but he needs both hands to hold on. His bare feet struggle for a grip against the side of the house.

Uh oh. The pipe's even looser than last summer. It rattles something fierce! But maybe his mama won't wake up. It could be a squirrel or a bird. He hopes.

There. He's on the ground, hurrying to the big pine, his shadow flying like a black ghost in the moonlight. He sets The Doubler down real careful, on the far side of the trunk. He growls out the charm, just like he planned. Then he scrambles, mostly quietly, back up the pipe. Mission accomplished!

Jerry listens carefully. No sound at all from downstairs. His mama must be sleeping like a baby.

SIX

SUNDAY morning, at the kitchen table, Jerry is so excited he barely notices his mama pouring ketchup onto his steaming-hot waffles.

Did The Doubler work? How can he sneak it into the house before they leave for church? If only he could run like The Flash . . . or make himself invisible like The Shadow!

Jerry's mama works her teabag like a little yo-yo. "Did you hear anything unusual last night?" she asks, a little too casually.

Jerry freezes, a hunk of red waffle halfway to his mouth. She heard him! And now she's trying to smoke something out! "Uh, no, Mama. I don't think so." He chomps on the waffle so he can't say more.

"Well, I did." His mama's eyes shine like twin lights. "And I know exactly what it was."

Jerry freezes like a deer in her headlights. "Wh-What, Mama?"

She leans forward, lowering her voice. "Your papa's

ghost, honey. Rattling the drainpipe. I'm almost sure of it."

Jerry's eyes stretch wide. He didn't expect that! "How . . . how do you know, Mama?"

"I'm no fool, dear." She takes a sip of tea. "Ghosts can rattle things, you know. Angry ghosts, I mean. And he must have been mighty angry to get shot in the War."

His mama shivers sadly. "No earthly way the wind could have rattled that drainpipe. There was only a gentle breeze. He did it twice too, to make sure I heard. I just lay there, trembling all over." She wipes away a sudden tear. "It's his way of apologizing . . . I was always nagging him to fix that drainpipe." Now she's sobbing into her napkin.

"It's okay, Mama." Jerry is trying not to cry too. "He's probably a happy ghost."

She lowers her napkin. "You think so, honey? I— Oh, I'll be right back." She jumps up and rushes from the room.

His mama suffers from "constipewshun," and she eats a lot of prunes. Sometimes too many prunes. Now's his chance!

Unlocking the kitchen door, Jerry races across the backyard to the pine. He grabs the box and flies upstairs to his room. A quick glance reveals more money. Seven dollars now. The magic worked! Stashing The Doubler deep in his closet, he hurries back down to the kitchen. Just in time, too.

His mama returns, a satisfied smile on her face. "Success," she declares. "If I hear your papa's ghost every night, I'll say good-bye to prunes. Scared it right out of me, hee hee. I'm gonna listen for him tonight. Listen like a hawk."

Jerry shudders. How will he use The Doubler?

His mama glances up at the kitchen clock. "Heavens! It's time to leave for church. Maybe your papa's ghost will be there, smiling down on us."

Jerry nods. He's deep in higher math. He pictures The Doubler with the lid partway open. It's so stuffed with dollar bills, it won't even close! How much will it hold? If it keeps on doubling his money . . .

* * *

Jerry sits beside his mama in an otherwise empty wooden pew, though the church is pretty full. His body quietly perches there, but his mind is soaring high in clouds of sunlit gold. He'll do it! Just a few extra doubles. One time after 28 will make 56 bucks. Two times, 112.

He vaguely remembers something Mr. Filkins said in arithmetic class about the power of doubling. How the Emperor of India promised to give a man some rice . . . Yes, it started with one grain of rice on the first square of a chessboard—and kept on doubling for all sixty-four squares. It added up to so much, the Emperor couldn't pay. And now, Jerry has that amazing power!

Preacher Plutz drones on and on. He waves away

an ambitious fly that circles and settles on his spread-open Bible. He's saying something about "spiritual goods" being superior to "worldly goods." People fidget and yawn.

Jerry's eyes have a bright, dreamy gleam. In his feverish mind, he's already doubled his money to 224, 448, and 896 dollars. And that's just three more nights. After that, the figuring is difficult, but 896 is almost a thousand, so he goes two thousand, then 4–8–16–32 thousand dollars. That's a fortune! In under two weeks. Wilcox doesn't seem to care much about time, so maybe he won't notice . . .

Suzie Steele, sitting across the aisle with her parents, adjusts her golden curls. Then she turns and flutters her dark eyes at Jerry. But he doesn't smile back like he usually does. Her face goes sour. Soon she turns the other way and smiles at Willie Fielder. His eyes light up, and he smiles back.

Preacher Plutz seems full of endless energy today. The congregation begins to nod and doze. Jerry is vaguely aware that the words "holy ghost" were uttered, and that his mama, beside him, suddenly twitched. But he's busy making tremendous money in his mind. What if he stretched it to sixty-four thousand? Glory be! He grins a greedy, dreamy grin.

His face suddenly falls. All that money wouldn't fit in The Doubler, would it? Wait! Maybe it would magically "make change" in a weird, reverse way, upping the green stuff to twenties, fifties, hundreds, thousands.

Then it would fit! He could pay all his mama's overdue bills. And he could buy so many things he's always dreamed about . . .

Jerry feels a sudden chill. He remembers the Wonderworker's words. *It's fine to make dough. Not if you're shady, though.* And Wilcox said only three doubles. *Don't try to fry your fish in the sky.* Jerry shivers in the warm, sleepy church. *Keep your intentions pure.* Helping his mama was a pure intention, but crossing Wilcox was certainly wrong. Maybe The Doubler was set to work for only three nights, and after that, it would set off some kind of alarm in the Wonderworker's headband. No, that was crazy! Or was it?

Slam! Several people jump, snapping out of their dozes. The fly had boldly returned, landing right on the Bible, and Preacher Plutz slammed it shut.

Jerry squirms. It's not right to kill a fly that way, is it?

The preacher smiles triumphantly. He has silenced the annoying fly and awakened his dozing congregation, all with a single blow. He's clearly pleased with himself. Now his pudgy fingers pull the heavy Bible open. He blows away the fly's remains (it takes two hard puffs, plus a fingernail flick) and continues his sermon.

Jerry looks sideways at his mama. She also seems troubled that he killed the fly that way. Very troubled. Almost like the fly was a living person.

SEVEN

LEAVING the church, Jerry is barely aware of Suzie Steele, looking puzzled out of the corners of her eyes. She had enjoyed smiling at Willie Fielder, to punish him for ignoring her. But she's tired of that now, and Jerry's still acting like she doesn't exist! What did she do to deserve this?

Jerry strides beside his mama, haunted by two huge, ghostly numbers: thirty-two thousand and sixty-four thousand. He knows it's wrong even to imagine them. But they seem to peer out at him from behind every building and bush, like those "Imps of Temptation" the preacher was talking about.

"He was there, Jerry." His mama shakes his arm. "I know it!"

"Huh? What, Mama? Who was there?"

"Your papa, of course." She smiles mysteriously. "I could feel his ghost was there all through the sermon."

Jerry squints in the bright sun. "I dunno, Mama. That's pretty—"

"I *do* know, honey," she interrupts. "I think he even used that fly . . . to get our attention."

Jerry's mouth drops open. "Mama! What are you saying?"

"Spirits can do that, you know. They use the eyes of living creatures to see us better. To watch us closely. It's called a medium. Yes, that poor fly was your papa's medium until . . ." She shudders, grimacing.

"But Mama. Then why did the fly circle around Preacher Plutz? Why didn't it come over to us?"

"That's just it, Jerry. Your papa's spirit knew we were focusing on the preacher, listening to his sermon. That was the most sacred way to get our attention. Your papa was probably enjoying the sermon, too."

Jerry rolls his eyes. "Mama, I think maybe—"

"You're too young, honey. To know about such things, I mean. I'm gonna confirm it, too. You just wait!"

They walk the rest of the way home in silence.

For lunch, "Henri" fixes a big pot roast with peas and mashed potatoes.

"Enjoy it, dear," Jerry's mama tells him. Our money isn't going to last forever. The expenses of this mansion are just too big. I don't know what we can do. Money doesn't grow on trees, you know."

No, but it does grow under trees, Jerry thinks to himself.

His mama is still talking. "If it did, we could just go

outside and pick some, like apples. But the bills keep piling up, and my salary at The Palace isn't exactly gigantic." (She works at a beauty parlor called The Pretty Palace.)

Jerry's mouth is full. "I know, Mama. I've got a plan for making money."

"Oh, no, dear! You're still too young. We'll manage." She wipes away a tear. "I shouldn't carry on so. Your papa used to say there are two reasons people talk a lot. One is to spread their ignorance. The other is to cover up their ignorance." She takes a sip of tea and sighs. "But there's one more. To cover up their sadness. Remember how your papa used to read you that little baby book? *Howard The Happy Basset Hound.* You loved his floppy ears. You used to giggle like you were being tickled! Your papa giggled too. And then he'd hug you and kiss your sweet little squirming cheek."

"Uh, Mama, I think you're bringing it all back."

She looks startled. "Oh, sorry, honey. I suppose you're right. I won't say anything more about it."

Jerry barely hears her. He's weakly resisting temptations to keep on doubling his money after the third time. And he's trying to think about what he'll do tonight, at midnight. He's got to sneak past his mama somehow. And she's going to be listening "like a hawk."

EIGHT

AFTER lunch, Jerry's mama rushes out, saying she'll be back in time for supper. She looks very intent on something, like it can't wait at all.

Jerry is deep in his own thoughts. He can't figure out what to do tonight! So he decides to sneak away and ask the Wonderworker.

He moves stealthily through the woods, nervous and alert. He's careful not to step on any dry sticks. He keeps whipping his head around until his neck is sore. No one follows him.

As usual, Wilcox is sitting cross-legged beside his cardboard house. As usual, he's wearing his faded red headband. As usual, he raises his hand while his eyes are still closed. "Turnip! What brings you here this fine afternoon?"

"Uh, hi, Wonderworker. The Doubler worked!"

Wilcox opens his eyes. He gives Jerry a warm smile. "I knew it was a good one, the moment I saw it." His magic hands make curving swoops, like dolphins diving in the air. "Have a seat, young magician." He pats the grass beside him.

Young magician! Wow! Maybe he is. Jerry sits down, unsure how to begin. "I've got seven dollars now. But . . ."

"But what, Magic Turnip?" Wilcox strips off his headband. He slips it through his fingers, and it turns dark purple.

As usual, Jerry gapes. "I've got two nights to go. And it's not easy . . . keeping The Doubler a secret. My mama heard me sliding down the drainpipe last night."

The Wonderworker blows on his headband, and it's red again. "Why don't you try something different?"

"That's the problem." Jerry rearranges his butt on the long, dry grass. "I don't know what to do. She's such a light sleeper."

Wilcox nods. "You'll need to be very quiet." He swishes his headband through the air, and it disappears!

"How . . . how did you do that?"

"My headband's feeling rambunctious today." The Wonderworker laughs. "Hold still." He reaches over and pulls it out of Jerry's ear! Jerry can almost feel it coming out. He stares. The headband is wriggling like a fresh-caught fish.

Wilcox ties it back on. "So," he says thoughtfully. "The headband did something different. You'll have to do something different too."

"But what? My mama's going to listen . . . like a hawk. That's what she said.

"Why, Magic Turnip?"

Jerry squirms. "Do you believe in ghosts?"

Wilcox raises his eyebrows. "Ghosts! Now that's a complicated subject. What makes you ask?"

"When my mama heard me on the drainpipe last night, she, uh, thought it was my papa's ghost."

The Wonderworker gives him a long, hard look. "Really?"

"Yes. She said she used to nag him to fix it, so that's why he rattled it. She thinks he was apologizing for not fixing it."

The Wonderworker nods. "Well, we know who rattled the drainpipe, don't we?" He gives Jerry another long, piercing look. "But it's possible that your papa's ghost returned."

Jerry is stunned. Ghosts are real! He's never really believed in them. He always thought they were scary made-up stuff, like monsters and trolls and goblins. "What do ghosts do?"

Wilcox clears his throat. "I can't really say. I don't recall being one." He laughs like he's just told a funny joke. But then his face turns serious. "When we die, what happens depends . . . on how we've prepared for it."

Jerry stares. "What do you mean?"

The Wonderworker looks dreamily into the distance. "When you die and leave your body behind, something amazing happens. A hidden being, a part of you that has carefully observed your entire life, touches your consciousness. That being . . . is your Higher Self. Through its eyes, you can see how you lived, what you did with the gift of your life. You get to see . . . how you used the opportunity. And sometimes it's possible to communicate with people who are still alive. But usually it doesn't happen."

Jerry's head is spinning. "What . . . usually does happen? I thought everybody went up to Heaven or down to Hell."

Wilcox nods. "And which way is up?"

"What do you mean?"

"Well, you said *up to Heaven,* but the world is spinning. What's up right now is down twelve hours later. Maybe it's not a question of up or down. Maybe our next location is outside of space and time."

Jerry stares. "How could that be?"

The Wonderworker smiles. "To twist the words of a great poet, there may be more dimensions than are dreamt of in your philosophy." He makes magic passes with his hands. "After you die, and have mentally digested your life, I think you rest in a deep sleep . . . in another dimension . . . to prepare for your return to Earth."

Jerry gulps. "As a ghost?"

"No. In your next body. You return for another

chance. I happen to believe we keep getting reborn . . . until we live this life right. So coming back is not a vicious circle. It's a rising spiral." Wilcox gets that dreamy, distant look again. "Your next life is determined by forces, called karmic forces, that are formed by how you lived this one—and any lives before it."

Jerry's eyes are wide. "I've lived . . . other lives?"

Wilcox smiles. "Very many. Everyone has."

"Jiggers! How come I can't remember them?"

"If you remembered everything that happened in all your past lives, you might get them mixed up with this one." Wilcox laughs. "Actually, some people do recall a few things."

Jerry gasps. "Do you?"

The Wonderworker slides his headband down over one eye. "Sometimes I seem to remember being a pirate. Avast, ye landlubbers!" He slashes the air with an imaginary sword, grinning viciously.

Jerry gapes. Maybe Wilcox really is crazy! But he's right about a lot of things. Jerry has no idea what to believe. "My papa was killed in the War. Mama says he was probably angry when he got shot. Is that why he's a ghost?"

The Wonderworker sighs. "It's possible. Who knows? But I'm sure he wouldn't object to your using The Doubler. He'd be very happy that you're trying to do . . . what is honest and true."

Jerry smiles. "I am, but it's not easy."

"Don't worry." He looks deeply into Jerry's eyes. "Your Higher Self can help you in ways you can't even imagine."

Jerry nods knowingly. "Thanks, Wonderworker!" He feels much better. The Wonderworker is hinting that he's giving him some magic help.

Jerry doesn't say a word about his plan to use The Doubler more than three times. "Well, I gotta get back, or Mama will be worried."

NINE

UP in his room, Jerry stares grimly at his history book. The print swims and looks shimmery, like it's under water. The letters treacherously turn into numbers, like 32 and 64. Even 128. *Don't try to fry your fish in the sky.* He stares away the numbers. For some reason, he remembers his Higher Self.

Downstairs, his mama is busy fixing supper. She got home just after he did. Thanks, Wonderworker!

Jerry keeps trying to concentrate. Who cares what caused the Roman Empire to collapse? What matters is how he's going to sneak The Doubler out at midnight. Like a hawk, she said. Even if the drainpipe doesn't pull away from the house and fall, it will rattle. Then she'll come running for sure, with her hair streaming out behind her nightie, like the time a tree branch broke the living room window in the big storm . . . Hey! Jerry's eyes light up. Why didn't he think of that before? He's got a new plan now.

When he comes down to supper, there's a funny smell in the kitchen. His mama's stirring a big pot, humming happily.

Jerry sniffs in the fumes, slowly breathes them out. "Mushroom soup? You haven't made that since . . ."

"I know. Since your papa left us. But he's back now." She smiles. Her eyes are all watery, like she's in a trance. "I went to see Sister Sorsy, and she confirmed it! She looked into her crystal ball."

"Mama, what do you mean?" Jerry knows all about Sister Sorsy. Her real name is Hilda Snekburt. She wears long robes and a turban. Sits at a little round table with her crystal ball. People actually pay her to do "mystical readings." The kids at school say she's a kook.

"What I mean is," his mama draws herself up tall, "Sister Sorsy says your papa's spirit *probably* rattled the drainpipe and *very possibly* watched us through the eyes of that fly. She advised me to cook one of his favorite foods, adding vinegar to make the aroma stronger, and you know how your papa loved mushroom soup. I had to do this by myself, so I gave Henri the night off."

"But why, Mama?"

"He might have messed it up. I know just how your papa liked it. Thick and creamy with—"

"No, Mama. Why cook the soup for papa?"

"Haven't got much otherworldly sense yet, do you? To signal him that we *know*, of course. He can smell it, even if he can't taste it. To show him that we care, and we're lovingly ready for his next appearance. That's what Sister Sorsy said, *lovingly ready*. And that's why I'm gonna listen like a hawk tonight."

Jerry shudders. But then he thinks it over. His plan can still work, if he carries it out perfectly.

They eat their cornflakes and cinnamon buns in edgy silence. Jerry's mama thinks for a minute, then adds a few dried prunes to her bowl, just in case the spirit doesn't appear.

All of a sudden, Jerry lets out a loud gurgle-burp.

"Heavens, honey! Where did your manners go?"

"Disappeared, I guess. Must be magic!"

"Don't you sass me, young man."

"Sorry, Mama."

After supper, Jerry lies on the rug in the darkened living room near the big radio. The name "Zenith" has a cool, lightning-shaped Z. He's listening to The Shadow. His mama doesn't approve ("It's much too scary, dear!"), but tonight she's busy fussing with her soup and doesn't object at all. The radio dial has a warm, eerie glow.

The weed of crime bears bitter fruit. The Shadow knows! Then comes a shivery, nasty laugh. It sounds much better in the darkness.

Tonight's crooks are plotting to kill a helpless old lady and make it look like an accident. They think they're alone, but Lamont Cranston (The Shadow) has probably clouded their minds so they can't see him.

Jerry likes to imagine The Shadow, lurking near the scheming crooks. He's invisible and absolutely quiet, so he's only there when Jerry pictures him. Sort of like the way memories of his papa float inside his mind, ready to be imagined.

*   *   *

In bed, coiled on his side, Jerry finally sees a quarter of twelve on his nightstand clock! That's the time he planned on for tonight. This time, it will probably take a little longer. Snatching up The Doubler (containing seven dollars now), he stuffs it under his pajama shirt. Inside, with the money, there's a piece of paper with "Thank you!" carefully printed on it. Do magical objects like to be thanked? Jerry doesn't know, but people certainly do. Anyway, how can it hurt?

Taking a deep breath, he eases himself out of bed. The springs *sproing* loudly, but he could have just been rolling over. At least, that's what he hopes.

He tiptoes barefoot to the door, quietly pulling it open. Jiggers! He forgot that squeaky floorboard in the hall. He freezes, listening. He doesn't dare breathe. It's amazing how the smallest noise can travel through a house at night.

He's lucky so far. No sound from below. He starts creeping slowly down the stairs. He stays close to the wall, where the steps don't creak as much, but the third one makes a treacherous noise.

Slowly, quietly. The house is cool, but sweat is rolling down his face, dripping from his nose. His pajamas stick to his arms and legs.

Oh, no! His mama's door swings open. She'll catch him for sure!

But she's rushing to the bathroom. Could prunes work that fast? Maybe she thought she heard his papa's ghost. She's "lovingly ready," but probably scared too. Jerry is pretty scared himself.

The bathroom door clicks shut. Now's his chance! He tiptoes into the living room, pads across the thick, silent rug. There's moonlight, so he easily dodges the furniture. Reaching the window, he cautiously slides it open. Why didn't he think of this the first night?

As Jerry races across the yard, the night air chills his sweaty face. His bare feet sink into the soft, cold ground. Now he leaves The Doubler under the pine and growls out the magic charm. Has his mama finished? If not, it'll be easy. If she's on the way back to her room, she'll catch him.

Sneaking back in through the open window, he hears the toilet flush. It's loud, a perfect cover. He races back up the dark stairs. As he opens his door, he hears the bathroom door open down below. Perfect timing. Now he can go back to—Oh, no! He forgot to close the window!

TEN

JERRY floats slowly up to the surface of his consciousness. He's been dreaming about Suzie's golden curls, lit by a shaft of sunlight through the church window. She was smiling at Willie Fielder, and Jerry was about to hit Willie over the head with a heavy Bible.

"Jerry! You awake? This is the second time I've called you! It's Monday. Hurry or you'll be late for school!"

"Yes, Mama! I'll be right down." He's never dressed so fast in his life. When he reaches the kitchen, the air is heavy with mushroom soup.

His mama gives him a plate of burnt French toast, dripping with melted butter, honey, *and* syrup. She looks sleepy and worried.

"Did you hear anything last night, dear?"

"Uh, no, Mama." He thinks of Wilcox, and quickly adds: "I didn't hear papa's ghost at all. Maybe he didn't—"

"Oh, he did! He came to see us. He left the living room window wide open! It couldn't have been a thief, because nothing is missing." She wipes away a tear. "But I didn't hear a thing. I listened so hard, too. Guess I must have dozed off for a few minutes." She yawns, takes a long sip of tea. "But I swear I don't remember falling asleep or waking up. Jade didn't hear him either."

Jerry chews a bite of gooey burnt toast. "I guess ghosts can be very quiet, Mama."

"You're right, dear. I looked all over, but he didn't leave any sign for us. Poor thing! Probably used up all his strength opening the window. He always opened that window when he smoked his pipe." She wipes away more tears. "I knew he'd come to smell the mushroom soup."

Jerry slams down his fork. "I think I heard something in the cellar!"

"What? What was it, dear?"

"Oh, probably just a mouse."

"No! Jade gets them all. You stay here." Snatching the soup pot from the stove, she rushes down the cellar stairs.

But Jerry doesn't stay. He's already racing across the yard, snatching up The Doubler, dashing up the stairs to his room. Wow! Fourteen dollars. And his thank-you note is gone. The Doubler swallowed it! An eerie thrill runs down his spine.

Jerry runs back down to the kitchen, where his mama sits with her head in her hands. "I was too late, dear. If your papa's spirit was there, he'd already left. But you mark my words. I'll hear him tonight if it's the last thing I do! I'm gonna stay in the living room all night."

＊　＊　＊

A lot of guys are waiting near the school when Jerry walks up. All the guys who paid to use The Viewer. They must have had a conference or something over the weekend.

"Hey, Jerry!" Cromer Borkin waves a meaty hand. "How's The Viewer doin'? Activatin' yet?" He blocks Jerry's path, folding his muscular arms across his chest.

"Yeah," says Willie Fielder. "I think you've been conning us. I seen you stuffin' yer face with ice cream sodas. Spendin' *our* money."

Jerry takes a few steps back, but he's surrounded now. "Easy, guys. I think it's almost ready."

"You think?" Cromer slams Jerry's shoulder so hard, he almost falls over backwards. "Make it work . . . or give us our money back. Now!"

Jerry fixes him with a cold, powerful gaze. Unfortunately, The Look has no effect at all. "The Viewer will activate soon, I swear."

"Oh, yeah?" says Willie. "What makes you so sure, twinkle toes?"

"Yeah, fairy!" says Cromer. "You're sweet on Monty, haw haw."

Jerry shudders inside. His only real friend, now that he's dealing in magical objects, is Monty Flowers, a mouse-like boy with a bad lisp. Jerry recently saved him from getting beat up by Cromer. Somehow he managed to talk Cromer out of it. He promised him an extra long look through The Viewer. A hint about his magic powers also helped.

Of course, Jerry really has a crush on Suzie Steele, but he doesn't want anyone to know. "One more day," he says, smiling mysteriously. If The Viewer doesn't activate by then, everybody gets their money back. I promise."

Willie hesitates. He doesn't dare push too hard, because some of Jerry's magic powers might be real. "All right. Tomorrow, but that's all."

Cromer reluctantly agrees.

Soon the last bell rings, and they all troop slowly into the school.

ELEVEN

IN the school cafeteria, Jerry eats lunch with Monty Flowers. The small, mouse-like boy is wearing stupid, baggy brown overalls. They match his stupid Buster Brown shoes.

"Are you gonna pay the money back?" Monty asks. "If The Viewer doesn't activate?"

"Yeah," says Jerry. "I guess so. But maybe it'll work by tomorrow. You wanna use it when it does?"

Monty doesn't get to answer. Willie Fielder unexpectedly barges over and clanks down his lunch tray. "Okay if I sit with you guys?"

"Sure." Jerry shrugs.

"Yeth," says Monty.

At that moment, a commotion breaks out across the room. It's Cromer Borkin and Peter Wardly. They fling scooped-up hunks of mashed potatoes at each other. They fill their mouths with peas and blow in each other's faces. They call each other loud, disgusting names.

While everyone stares, Willie slyly slips something into Jerry's glass of chocolate milk.

Now Peter flips over Cromer's lunch tray! With an angry roar, Cromer jumps up and pushes Peter over backwards. Shouting loudly, they snarl and shove each other.

Laughing strangely, Willie eggs them on.

Monty, whose darting, mouse-like eyes saw what Willie did, quickly swaps milk glasses between Jerry and Willie.

Almost as abruptly as it started, the brawl subsides. Mr. Flog, the principal, looms in the doorway.

"I guess the fight is over," Willie declares. "Let's drink a toast."

"Why?" asks Jerry.

"It's fun!" says Willie. "Especially a Russian toast. You've gotta toss it back real hard."

"Show uth," says Monty.

Willie snorts. "You guys don't know nuttin', do ya? Watch this!" He lifts his glass of chocolate milk and takes a forceful slug. "Ow!" He covers his mouth with one hand. He spits out a long shower of dark liquid and . . . a marble that bounces and rolls across the table.

Jerry stares.

Monty nods and grins.

Suzie Steele suddenly appears beside their table. "You said to watch Jerry drink his chocolate milk, Willie. But you're the one who put on a show!" She smiles at Jerry and walks away.

Willie's face is a nightmare of rage and pain. He goes off to the restroom to see if his front teeth are cracked.

"Therves him right," Monty declares.

"What did Suzie mean by that?" Jerry wonders out loud.

Monty says nothing. His eyes sparkle.

"Did you put that marble in Willie's glass?"

Monty smiles. "No. Willie did."

"What? He put the marble in his own chocolate milk?"

"Yeth. But it was your milk then." Monty grins. "I switched glathes."

Jerry's eyes widen. "Thanks, Monty! You saved my butt."

Soon Willie returns to the table, one hand over his mouth. "You . . . You broke my tooth!" he sputters at Jerry. "I'll get you for that. You changed glasses."

"I didn't," says Jerry. But then he glances at Monty, who's looking down meekly at his lunch tray. Monty's his friend. Monty saved him!

"I didn't," Jerry repeats. "I used magic to cloud your mind. You put the marble in your own glass. You broke your own tooth."

Willie glares in amazement. "You never!" he cries. "That's a load of bull, and you know it!" But his voice cracks a little as he says this. He angrily slinks away.

TWELVE

AFTER school, the kids pour out of the building like it's on fire. They yawn, stretch, and sigh.

Standing at the bottom of the steps, Jerry throws back his shoulders, smoothes his hair. Then he walks over to Suzie: "Okay if I walk you home?"

She looks at him sideways. "Sure. Why not?"

They follow the sidewalk slowly, each one not quite looking at the other. After a while, Suzie says: "What were you thinking about in church yesterday?"

Jerry smiles. "Ways to make money."

Suzie laughs. "Like robbing a bank?"

"No. Legal ways." He takes a deep breath, and suddenly, out it comes. "Will you marry me?"

Suzie gasps. "You're kidding."

"Nope. Will you?"

"We're only ten, Jerry."

"I don't mean now, silly. When we're older, after I make a lot of money."

Suzie stops abruptly. They're almost opposite her house. "You're serious?"

"Yep." He's encouraged. At least, she didn't say no!

Suzie flutters her eyes. "Ask me then," she says. "When you're rich, manly, and handsome."

"I'm not manly and handsome now?"

"Almost." She laughs and skips away toward her house.

*　　*　　*

When Jerry gets home, he's hit by a blast of fresh mushroom soup, generously laced with vinegar.

"Hi, honey!" his mama calls cheerfully. "Guess who's coming for a visit to our mansion tonight."

Jerry rolls his eyes before he can hide the reaction. "Uh, I think I know, Mama."

"Of course you do. Now scamper upstairs and do a wonderful job on your homework. Your papa will be delighted to see you hard at work, if he floats into the house a little early." She smiles smugly. "By the way, Sister Sorsy said it was *entirely possible* that your papa opened the window. Ghosts with strong emotions sometimes display amazing strength."

Up in his little room, Jerry really does try to focus. But he's dreaming, as usual, of higher math. His hands shake while he pencils another "Thank you!" on another piece of paper. Now he lays the note carefully atop the fourteen dollars.

Closing The Doubler, he can almost hear the voice

of Crazy Wilcox: "Be sure . . . your intentions are pure." But if his intentions are to help his mama, isn't that pure enough? What does his Higher Self think about that?

Deep in his heart, he knows that he also wants some of the extra money for himself. He's got his eye on a lot of games and toys at Woolworth's. Jerry scowls and bites his tongue.

"Ready, honey!" his mama calls. "Soup's on, so to speak, hee hee."

Jerry feels relieved. He can stop thinking for a while about a few extra doubles. "I'll be right down, Mama!"

In the kitchen, you can almost cut the mushroom-soup fumes with a knife.

"We're having leftover rot post." His mama giggles. "Rot post! I gave Henri and Clara the night off." She lowers her voice. "I think they went on a date, hee hee."

Jerry laughs in spite of himself. "They won't get to see papa."

"That's right, dear." His mama pulls some steaming bread from the oven. "Your papa might be a little shy. He never did like large gatherings."

The pot roast tastes even better the second time. Jerry dips his bread in the gravy and sighs. "This is good, Mama."

"Glad you like it. Henri's a super chef. How did school go?"

Jerry thinks back. Here's something he can tell her.

"It was funny, Mama. Somebody slipped a marble into Willie Fielder's chocolate milk. You should have heard him howl when it hit his teeth!"

"Land's sakes! A marble? What you kids don't think up! Who would do such a thing? What if he'd swallowed it?"

Jerry pauses, considering what she might do if she knew what Monty told him. "I didn't see who did it, Mama." This was perfectly true. "But somebody said it would have come out all right in the end."

His mama laughs. Then her face goes deadly serious. "Well, tonight's the night! I'm lovingly ready. I'm gonna sit in your papa's favorite chair by the open window with the lights out. And listen like a hawk."

The gravy-soaked bread turns sour in Jerry's mouth. He's been mentally scanning his options. No more drainpipe. The window's out too. She'll be wide-awake, sitting beside it. And the doors make noise. But Wilcox said to keep it a secret, or the magic won't work!

"Did you hear me? You look like you're fifty miles away!"

"Uh, yes, Mama. Like a hawk." Hey! There was a big bird perched on a branch, while he was doing his homework. That maple tree practically touches his window. Why didn't he think of it before? Maybe Wilcox magically sent the bird, to give him an idea!

"I heard you, Mama. Like a hawk."

THIRTEEN

JERRY is lying on his side, staring endlessly at the luminous face of the clock. Time flies, some people say, but it's not flying now.

Once his papa said: "Time flies. I cannot. They go in and out so rapidly." Jerry couldn't make sense of that, no matter how hard he tried. Finally, his papa explained that he was talking about *timing* flies, to see how fast they fly!

At last, the big hand inches ahead. The clock shows twenty of twelve. Close enough. The house is absolutely quiet, but he can picture his mama downstairs, sitting in the big chair listening.

Easing himself out of bed, Jerry grabs The Doubler and slips it under his pajama shirt. He tucks in the shirt, pulling the drawstring of his pajama bottoms painfully tight. That will hold the box. He's going to need both hands free now. He's not Tarzan!

His window, already open a crack, slides quietly the rest of the way. Then he focuses on the big maple branch just outside. Unfortunately, it's not exactly just outside. The flimsy end of the branch is close, but it's all twigs and leaves. So he'll need to jump. Jump big. But he knew that, even though he hadn't totally admitted it yet.

Squatting on the window ledge, Jerry takes a deep breath. Then he springs into space, catching the big branch with both hands. Whoa! It bends waaay down. It looked much stronger than that. But it's a young tree, and the branch bends down halfway to the ground. He's dangling frantically in midair! He grits his teeth and lets go.

Hitting the ground, he rolls like a commando. Above him, the branch swishes back up into place. At least, it didn't break. That would have brought his mama for sure! He lies quietly in the grass, cradling the precious box against his stomach like a football. He listens fearfully. The crickets are buzzing in the shadowy, moonlit darkness.

A miracle! His mama doesn't react. Maybe Wilcox put a sleep spell on her, and she's dozing.

Jerry springs to his feet, races over to the pine, and deposits The Doubler, growling out the magic charm.

Now what? He can climb back up the tree, all right, but that branch is much too springy to let him get close to his window. Now he's trapped outside. Does he have to wait until morning? And if he does, how will he explain being out of the house?

In desperation, Jerry sneaks around the house on tiptoe. He peeks in the open window. He can see the shape of his mama, sitting in the dark. Her head is bent to one side. She's snoring softly. Wilcox did put a sleep spell on her!

Very carefully, he climbs in. If he bumps anything, she'll wake up for sure. He's so close, he could touch her. He tiptoes very slowly past her chair. Uh-oh. She stirs in her sleep, moans something softly. Jerry freezes. He feels cold prickles all over.

Now she's quiet again, breathing deeply. He moves on.

Oh, no. Jerry feels a sneeze coming. A huge, powerful sneeze. He clamps both hands over his nose and mouth. But the sneeze *demands* to come out. And she's just behind him. He'll never make it. The jig is up!

"Hamuph!" It sounds so loud in the dark, quiet room! Quick as a flash, Jerry whirls around. He starts walking *toward* his mama. She's already sitting up and stretching.

"Hi," he whispers cautiously. "Are you okay?"

"Jerry!" She sounds wide-awake now. "What are you doing?"

"Are you okay?" he repeats. "I was hoping . . . you were asleep." That much is totally true! "Do you need anything?"

His mama sighs in the darkness. "No thanks, dear. I think I dozed off for a minute. You go back up to bed. Get some sleep. If your papa wants to see you, I'll call, I promise. But he may be too shy the first time."

"Yes, Mama. Good luck!" He lunges up the stairs, two at a time.

*   *   *

The next morning, Jerry's mama seems to be sleep-walking. Her face is puffy and her eyes are glazed. "No luck," she sadly declares. "I was almost certain your papa would come."

Jerry mumbles something encouraging, trying to make her feel better. But when she pours hot coffee on his corn flakes, he says: "Why don't you take a nap, Mama? I can finish getting breakfast for myself."

"Well, maybe I'd better." She's sloshing her orange juice now. Don't bother to clean up. Clara will do it." So saying, she shuffles off to her bedroom.

Dumping the coffee-soaked flakes in the trash, Jerry fixes himself a fresh bowl. Then, hearing some peaceful snores, he races out and grabs The Doubler.

Up in his room, he checks out the contents. Twenty-eight beautiful dollars! His thank-you note is gone. As before, The Doubler swallowed it.

Jerry briefly tries out The Viewer on his wall, but it acts like a regular old cardboard toilet paper roll. He'll have no choice but to give the money back. At least he's got it now. For some strange reason, he doesn't feel like using The Doubler for a few more nights. It feels good to be out of this mess, and good to be honest about it. Could that be the influence of his Higher Self?

*　　*　　*

When Jerry gets to school, the guys are waiting for him, like before. But this time, he's ready for them. "There's still a delay," he announces. "So I'll refund the money to anyone who wants it." He flips open the lid of what looks like an old cigar box.

Mouths drop open. Eyes bug out. Everyone crowds around him.

"Where'd you get this?" Peter suspiciously snarls.

"Yeah," says Cromer. "You steal it?"

"Maybe it's counterfeit," Willie suggests. "He already spent the cash we gave him."

Jerry manages to look surprised and offended. "I had some savings," he truthfully declares. "The money is real. Here, take a look."

The guys finger the bills, clink the change.

"Lookths real to me," says Monty, grinning in disbelief.

Cromer takes the first bill. "Thanks, Jerry. Sorry I had you figured wrong."

"Yeah," says Willie. "But that's a lotta savings." He sullenly grabs his two bucks.

Peter seems convinced, though he hesitates briefly. "I wish The Viewer did work," he declares. "I'd rather look through it than have this dollar."

Soon they've all got their money back. The Doubler is empty. Last bell rings, and everyone goes inside, still faintly suspicious of Jerry's sudden wealth.

In the classroom, Jerry slumps down onto his seat. It feels good to return the money, but he's sad that the magic didn't work. The Viewer would have been so cool! Why didn't it work . . . like The Doubler?

FOURTEEN

CLUTCHING The Doubler, Jerry heads directly for the junkyard. He's supposed to go straight home after school, but maybe his mama is still asleep. She was exhausted! Anyway, he needs to return The Doubler.

As usual, Jerry keeps looking over his shoulder. No one follows him, not even Monty. The walk through the woods is pleasant and warming. He takes slow, deep breaths. The Wonderworker will be proud of him. He—

Snap! Jerry freezes. What was that? He's been so careful! His eyes dart toward the sound, where a dark shape seems to disappear behind some thick, leafy bushes. He takes a few running steps, stops, listens closely. The only sound is the feathery swishing of leaves in the wind. Maybe it was just a stray dog, cracking a dry branch.

When Jerry gets to the junkyard, his eyes stretch wide. Wilcox is gone! So is his cardboard house. The entire world seems to collapse around Jerry. Everything else looks just the same: piles of trash, old, torn tires, wagon wheels, boxes, crates, broken bits of machinery.

But no Wilcox. No sign of Wilcox at all. He always goes South for the winter, but this is May. Jerry has a creepy feeling that it was all some kind of weird dream, that there never really was a Wonderworker, that he only imagined the whole thing, and—

"Hello, young friend!"

Jerry whirls around. Behind him, on a little hill in the woods, sits Wilcox. His cardboard house is up there, too.

Jerry's mouth drops open. He rushes up the hill, as if Wilcox might disappear if he doesn't hurry.

"Had to change locations," the old man declares. "They dumped some smelly stuff not far from my house. Fortunately, I don't have much to move." He thumps a cardboard wall. "Sit down, Turnip." He pats the leaves beside him.

"I brought The Doubler back," says Jerry, sitting down.

"I see you did, Turnip. Only kept it for three nights, too. Did it work?"

"Yes, thanks. I'm out of debt now. I think my Higher Self helped me."

The Wonderworker gives a radiant smile. "Splendid!" he exclaims. "At this rate, you may soon be able to recognize its presence."

"It gives presents?" asks Jerry.

Wilcox laughs. "You could put it that way. You can

feel that it's with you, always with you, ready to help."

"I'm glad," says Jerry. "I really needed help. The Viewer . . . never did activate."

Wilcox sighs. "Well, magic isn't always reliable." He reaches up and pulls something out of his headband. "And sometimes, there's a perfectly natural explanation." He holds out two pieces of paper.

Jerry gapes. The two notes he left in The Doubler! "You . . . you . . . gave me the money. The Doubler isn't real!"

"That's right, Turnip." Wilcox smiles. "Thought I'd help you out a little."

Jerry's world collapses once again. The Doubler was a fake. He had known it, but not known it, all along. "The guys better not find out about this!" he says. "They think the money was my savings."

"Don't tell them, then." The Wonderworker shrugs. "Does your mother know?"

"No." Jerry shakes his head. "I didn't tell her."

"Well, then she can't tell." Wilcox adjusts his magic headband. "You won't tell, and I won't tell. So how will they find out?" He almost shouts these last words, and Jerry jumps.

"I'll tell!" A gleeful voice rings out from behind a wide tree. And out steps Willie Fielder, a triumphant, murderous grin on his face.

Jerry's eyes bug out. "You . . . you followed me!"

Willie moves closer. "That's right, chump! I knew you were up to something, *Turnip*." He laughs a nasty laugh. "Didn't see me either, did you, bright boy?" He sticks a trembling finger in Jerry's face. "I knew you spent the money on Hershey bars, comics, strawberry sodas. I seen you do it. Wait till Cromer and the guys hear you got the money from Crazy Wilcox!"

Jerry is speechless. His head is filled with terrible visions of what will happen.

Willie dances over to the Wonderworker. "You crazy old fool!" he jeers. "What did Turnip do, cry in your lap? I'll tell everybody, everybody!"

"You dirty traitor!" Jumping up, Jerry rushes forward, both hands fisted.

"Wait." Wilcox springs to his feet and holds Jerry back. He turns to face Willie. "What will you say, my friend?" He looks coldly, deeply into Willie's angry eyes.

"I'll tell how you— Hey! Everything's spinning! I feel so dizzy!"

Wilcox catches Willie as he falls. "Steady," he says. "Things will soon quiet down." He eases Willie gently to the ground. "You'd better forget about what happened here . . . and go straight home."

"Yes." Willie is staring into space. "Yes, that's what I'd better do."

Jerry's eyes are wide. The Wonderworker is a genius!

Willie gets up slowly. He starts walking stiffly away.

"Wait." The Wonderworker takes him by the arms, looks into his eyes. "There's no need to act like a zombie." He smiles. "You must now be completely natural again. But you will forget that you followed Jerry here.

You will forget everything we did and said."

Willie focuses better now. "Yes, of course. I will. Good-bye."

They watch him disappear into the woods, never looking back at all.

Jerry turns to Wilcox. "You knew he was behind that tree, didn't you?"

The Wonderworker nods. "It's so quiet here, my ears are pretty sharp."

"Thanks for saving me," says Jerry. "The guys would have beaten me up real bad. Cromer pushes over old trees just for fun."

"Really? Tell me, Turnip. If a tree falls in the forest, and no one is there to hear it, does it make a sound?"

"Sure. Doesn't it?"

"Not unless someone creates it by hearing it."

Jerry gapes. "What do you mean?"

"I said no one was there, remember? No one to perceive the tree. No one to make it seem solid and real. Creatures from outer space might see and hear something totally different."

Jerry's mouth drops open. "You mean . . . they might see and hear in a different way?"

"Exactly." The Wonderworker smiles. "Your senses trick your brain into thinking that the tree is solid and independent. But it's not. Your experience of the tree is more like a wide-awake dream, so it seems real."

Jerry struggles to understand. "But my Higher Self is real, isn't it?"

FIFTEEN

THE WONDERWORKER holds Jerry by the shoulders, looks solemnly into his eyes. "Your Higher Self is fabulously real! And getting to know your Higher Self is the greatest happiness in the world."

"Whew." Jerry didn't expect to feel so relieved. He didn't realize how much it meant to him. "I know The Doubler was . . . a fake," he says. "But what about The Viewer? Will it ever activate?"

Wilcox shrugs. "Who can say? Ever is a very long time."

"But . . . but . . . if it's not real . . ."

The Wonderworker has a strange, distant look in his eyes. "Real?" he says dreamily. "As soon as we're born and open our eyes, Reality wears a convincing disguise." He sighs happily. He slips off his red headband. "Watch this." The headband vanishes.

"Where did it go?" asks Jerry.

"Right here." The Wonderworker slips it out of his sleeve. "Watch again."

This time, he palms it slowly, revealing the trick.

Jerry's eyes are wide. "That's cool!"

Wilcox nods. "It's called sleight of hand. My hand tricked you into thinking the headband disappeared. And when you perceive something, your brain is tricked into experiencing so-called reality. It could be called sleight of mind."

Jerry blinks. "So my mind is like a magician?"

"Right." The Wonderworker nods. "The mind creates everything you experience. That's the big magic." He smiles. "But merging with your Higher Self . . . is the biggest magic of all."

Jerry chews on this for quite a while. His head is swimming. "Can you help me do that? Merge with my Higher Self?"

"I'll try." The Wonderworker looks very serious. "If you keep coming back to see me this summer."

"I will!"

Jerry is silent for a few minutes. "So my magic objects were all tricks? Even The Bad-Dream Protector?"

Wilcox pulls on his scruffy beard. "That's hard to say. It partly depends on whether the user believes in it." He gets his faraway look. "God gives us the power to think and to feel, and clues to discover what's True and what's Real." He snaps his head, as if coming out of a trance. "Did you really believe the objects I gave you were magic?"

"Yes. At first, the magic was so much fun! And it

gave me power over the other guys . . . Then I wasn't sure. But I'd already taken the money, so I still hoped the magic was real."

Wilcox looks him in the eyes. "What were your intentions when you took the money for The Protector?"

Jerry squirms. "They weren't exactly pure. I can see that now."

"Well, maybe you should make amends. When you have enough money. You've come a long way, Turnip."

Jerry's face burns. "I guess maybe I have. I thought about using The Doubler a few more times, but I didn't. I didn't fry my fish in the sky."

Wilcox smiles. "I figured you might consider it." He waves Jerry's notes like two white birds. "But if you had, The Doubler would have gone smack empty. You'd have been dead broke."

Jerry shudders as it hits him. Cromer and the other guys would have beaten him to smithereens! He breathes a long sigh of relief. "Your headband doesn't really . . . whisper in your ear, does it?"

"What do you think, Turnip?"

"I . . . I don't know. Does it?"

The Wonderworker grins. "I don't know myself. Sometimes I think it does. But it's right beside my thinker, and maybe I get mixed up. Anyway, it gives me confidence. Sort of like those rusty-nail good-luck charms. Yes, that's it! The headband releases the power of my mind." He gives Jerry a deep, penetrating look, and the junkyard starts to swirl. "Your mind is a wonderful tool. But your intentions must be pure if you want magic results."

"The Look gets results!" says Jerry. "You just used it on Willie. But why didn't it work for me . . . except when I sold The Future Scope?"

The Wonderworker smiles. "The Look is a powerful form of hypnosis. So powerful, it might as well be magic. I taught you all about it . . . except for one little thing, which you must have stumbled upon by chance."

"There really is magic, then!" Jerry's all excited now. "But why didn't you teach me everything?"

"You weren't ready yet, Turnip." The Wonderworker sighs. "And you still aren't. But I can help you to prepare. Would you like that?"

"Would I!"

"Good. We'll work on it this summer. Now you must learn to meditate."

"Meditate?"

"Yes. First, you sit cross-legged. Good, but your hands stay like this. See how I do it? Right. Then you close your eyes and try not to think of anything. Now breathe deeply and slowly. Breathe out longer than you breathe in. Excellent! Do this every day, by yourself, for at least twenty minutes. Will you do that?"

"Sure."

The Wonderworker winks confidentially. "At first, it will be difficult not to think of anything. Thoughts keep popping up like confounded jackrabbits." His face suddenly turns serious. "But try to keep your mind still. Quiet but alert. Open to your Higher Self. Being open to love, goodness, and truth . . . invites the touch of the Divine."

He smiles happily. "Keep trying, Turnip. It's well worth it." His eyes get that dreamy look again. "Seek your inner stillness. Look deep enough, and you will find . . . your body is inside your mind."

"Huh?"

Wilcox points to where Willie was hiding. "Look at that tree. Good. Now, where is your mind?"

"In my head, I guess."

"No, that's your brain. Your mind contains both you and what you look at. Your mind is invisible, flexible, and potentially huge. It can reach to the stars."

Jerry struggles to understand. "I . . . I . . ."

"Don't worry. That will come later."

Jerry thinks for a minute. "Are you magic?" he asks. "Why?"

"I . . . I thought maybe you were using magic to help me use The Doubler and keep it secret. I had a lot of close calls."

The Wonderworker leans closer. "Maybe it was your Higher Self."

Jerry's eyes widen. "Does it do things like that too?"

The Wonderworker smiles. "Did you ever wonder why your hand found that concealed alarm button, years ago, in the bank? You told me you were lucky to hit it."

Jerry's eyes widen. "My Higher Self?"

"It's possible. Sometimes what seems like pure luck is really help from your Higher Self. It is the invisible fountain of your life force. It helps you in ways you can't imagine. Maybe you should be grateful to it."

"I will," says Jerry. "I mean, I am."

They sit quietly for a while. Suddenly Jerry jumps up. "Mama might be awake! She'll be worried. I've got to hurry home."

"Right, Turnip! Keep these as a reminder." Wilcox holds out the two little pieces of paper. "Your mind makes magic. Your heart knows truth." He hands the notes to Jerry. "Your Higher Self helps you go deep into your heart . . . and learn about your mind. Now go and help your mother."

Watching Jerry hurry away through the woods, the old man slowly adjusts his faded red headband.

SIXTEEN

WHEN JERRY NEARS HOME, his mama jumps up from her rocker on the porch. "Mercy! Where have you been? Are you all right?"

Jerry slumps down on the top step. "I, uh, stopped to see Wilcox."

"Oh, dear! I've told you so often to stay away from that man. What happened?"

Jerry buries his head in his hands. "I'm ashamed to say, Mama."

"What, honey, what?"

"My magical objects . . . I think they're all fakes." He's close to tears.

She puts her arm around him. "How do you know, dear?"

"Wilcox told me. He . . . admitted it."

"Dear me." His mama shakes her head.

"He, uh, gave me enough money to pay the guys. And now I have to pay the girls back too, for their rusty-nail charms."

His mama nods. "That might be a good idea, dear."

Jerry rubs his eyes. "Even the money I got paid for The Bad-Dream Protector."

"Don't worry, dear. Wilcox said—"

Her hand flies to her mouth, but it's too late.

The hair on Jerry's neck stands up. Suspicions skitter wildly through his mind. "You . . . You talked with Wilcox? You *know* him?"

"Well, I met him one day. We were both buying groceries, and—"

"You knew!" Once again, Jerry's world collapses. It was all a conspiracy. They were deceiving him!

"Let me explain, dear." She holds his arm to keep him from running away. "Listen, *please*. You were terribly upset when your papa died. We both were, remember?"

Jerry nods, glaring. He still can't believe it.

"Wilcox was a good friend to you. He distracted you, helped you get over the sadness. You broke a finger hitting the wall of your room. Remember? And you punched your pillow at night. I saw you doing it once. I tried to help, but I'm afraid I wasn't very good at it." She wipes away a tear. "Then Wilcox helped you with his magic. You did have fun, didn't you?"

"Well, sure, but . . . Hey! Why did you always tell me to stay away from him?"

His mama smiles sadly. "It's called negative

psychology, dear. If you want somebody to do something, just say Don't. Your papa used to say that without forbidden fruit, paradise wouldn't be paradise."

Jerry's mouth hangs open. "You and Wilcox were plotting together, all along!"

"Not really, dear. Just trying to help you feel better." She smiles. "When you were in school, Wilcox came over a few times for tea. Just to plan what was best for you."

Jerry gasps. That was how the Wonderworker knew about the big pine tree!

His mama sighs. "I was crushed when your papa died. I couldn't be a father for you too." She gives him a pleading look. "Please don't be angry with me. Wilcox and I thought . . . His magic objects were a diversion, to distract you from your loss, from your papa's death. He said to play along, but sometimes it wasn't easy. You were swindling all your friends, but Wilcox said to give it time. Your suffering was maturing you, he said. You were learning self-reliance. But you needed a diversion."

Jerry shakes his head. "You two were plotting to control me."

"Well, I guess so, dear. But it wasn't as bad as it sounds. The magical objects were sort of a joke to make you laugh, like Clara and Henri and Bodkins. But you're so persuasive. Your swindles were dangerously successful!"

"Mama, even when I was five, I knew the servants weren't real. I'm not an idiot."

"Of course you're not. You're smart as a whip. An idiot wouldn't have felt your papa's death . . . so keenly. Only five years old. Oh, what the good Lord makes us bear!"

Jerry puts his arms around his mama. "I know you helped me, Mama. Thank you!"

She hugs him back. "Oh, Jerry. I love you so much!"

They're both crying now. It feels good to hug and let the tears flow.

Finally, Jerry pulls back. "Mama, Wilcox wants me to see him a lot this summer."

"Why, dear?"

"He wants to teach me some things. Important things."

"Oh, that's wonderful!" She thinks for a moment. "If I *don't* tell you to stay away from him, will you still go?"

This time, they both laugh as they hug.

SEVENTEEN

THE SUMMER DAYS float slowly by, like fleecy clouds with golden edges. Some of the kids go away to camp. Others go on long vacations with their rich parents. A few, like Monty and Jerry, have jobs.

Jerry cuts grass and does weeding for two bossy old ladies. One tips him generously, and he gives money to his mama, but it's not enough. The bills just keep piling up. His mama stacks them according to urgency, with the most important bills on top.

One hot, humid afternoon, Jerry weeds until he's drenched with sweat, so the tipping lady will be extra generous. But she's furious! When she finally stops screeching and fussing, he learns that he pulled up her rare "prize" flowers by mistake. Some fancy Latin name. And they looked exactly like weeds! No blossoms or petals or anything. So now he only has one job.

Even worse, Jerry's mama loses her job at The Pretty Palace, unfairly, in an episode of beauty parlor intrigue.

Jerry notices that she eats less now, so that he can have plenty. "I'm just not hungry," she says. "But our money is running out. And the bank refuses to lend me any more." She sighs. "I'll have to let all the servants go. Jade doesn't like them tramping about, anyway. Her tail is never safe."

Jerry nods, smiling. But inside, he feels a hopeless ache.

*   *   *

The big bright spot in Jerry's life is his time with the Wonderworker. He visits Wilcox almost every day.

The sessions are more work than he expected, but fun too. Conversations about how to meditate. About right and wrong. About God too, infinity, and the universe.

Jerry learns to ruthlessly examine his own motivation and intentions. He looks into a mental mirror and sees a Jerry that makes him squirm a little. He feels like a detached detective, observing and tracking his own past crimes.

Jerry learns that his mind "thinks up" everything he experiences. Like the way a big Mind thinks the universe into being. And without his Consciousness, he would be unaware of the interaction between his seemingly real body and its seemingly real surroundings.

He also learns that Space and Time are strangely similar. Our solar system is moving through space, so if you could go back in time, you would go back in space as well! The universe is like a vast movie screen upon which space and time are projected. A screen set up inside infinity.

Jerry's Higher Self is where his own mind meets the infinite. And if he learns how to meditate better and better, he can master all his selfish desires and go deep inside, to a pure Stillness, where he can merge with his Higher Self!

At first it seems to take forever, but then he starts to enjoy it, almost like he's leaving Time behind! He savors reaching the inner Peace where troubles drop away. Once in a while, he gets the crazy but wonderful feeling that his Higher Self might be smiling. He smiles too. He feels like a wanderer, finally coming home.

Day after day, all summer long, Jerry meditates. A change gradually comes over his life, subtle but very real. He loves to watch a beautiful sunset. He listens with pleasure when his mama plays records of classical music. He even enjoys watching Jade, how she purrs and stretches and moves so gracefully.

During meditation, as he breathes deeply, the air seems cool and sweet. He feels humble and grateful for the joy that blossoms deep within.

*　　*　　*

One day, while Jerry leafs through comic books in Johnson's Pharmacy, he hears one man say to another: "Honesty is the best policy . . . 'cept when there ain't no profit in it." Both men chuckle and shake.

When Jerry tells Wilcox, the old man smiles. "Mark Twain, I think, once said something like that. It's funny, too, though a bit cynical."

Jerry thinks for a second. "Sinacle . . . So it's wrong?"

"Well, that depends. It's fine to make a profit if the deal is fair . . . and your motives are pure. But it's wrong to cheat or swindle." He clears his throat for emphasis. "Even if the other person agrees."

Jerry squirms. "I know that now," he says. "I'm really sorry about what I did. It was wrong, even if I hoped the objects really were magic." He pauses thoughtfully. "Peter Wardly said he'd rather use The Viewer than have his dollar back. But I shouldn't have told him it would work. At least, I returned the money. What did you call it? I made amends. It felt good to do that."

"Right." Wilcox looks deeply into Jerry's eyes. "I think you're ready, Turnip."

"Huh?" Jerry is still happy about making amends.

"Ready to learn the rest of The Look. But you must promise to use the power *only* to help others."

Jerry's eyes widen. "I promise!"

"Good. Never use it to take advantage of anyone. But if your heart tells you to stop someone with bad intentions, that is all right."

Jerry solemnly nods.

"Now. When you do The Look, gaze into the person's eyes as if you see right through them, as if you see their thoughts laid bare. Like this."

Jerry watches carefully, fighting off the dizziness.

"That's it!" he exclaims. "I was suspicious of that sales-man. I was afraid he'd sell Mama a set of phony gold brushes we couldn't afford. That was why it worked."

Wilcox grins. "Well, now you know." His face turns grimly serious. "The eyes are our most important sense organ. Maybe that's why they're set near the top of our heads. And your large, brown eyes are very sensitive. Perfect for seeing deeply into others. I think you may have been quite spiritually advanced in a previous life. But can you handle The Look . . . responsibly? Never use the power to play with others? Can you heed your Higher Self? Do what it guides you to do?"

Jerry feels proud that Wilcox is trusting him. "I . . . I think so. Yes!"

"Good. Now, here's one more thing. When you use The Look, it helps to think this magic word." He leans over and whispers in Jerry's ear. "That will activate The Look without fail. But you must have pure intentions in your heart." He pauses, smiling. "Do you remember I once told you that the road to hell is paved with good intentions?"

"Uh, yes. That was years ago."

"And that is why you must be absolutely sure . . . your intentions are pure?"

"Yes. I remember."

"Well, your Higher Self helps you to be sure."

For some reason, Jerry is very pleased to hear that. They sit in silence for a while. Gradually, Jerry hatches a secret plan.

EIGHTEEN

ONE late-August morning, just after nine, Jerry marches calmly into the bank. He's cool and serene on the outside, but there's a gang of wildcats snarling in his stomach.

The guard at the door looks him over carefully, like he's faintly suspicious. But he stands there stiffly and doesn't say a word.

Jerry walks straight to the nearest desk. Behind it sits a thin, severe lady who looks like she might snack on nails. Her fuzzy black sweater, draped across her shoulders, makes her resemble a perching vulture.

"Yes?"

"I'd like to see the president of the bank, please."

She smiles harshly, her beady eyes gleaming across the desk. "Do you have an appointment, sir?"

"Uh, no, but—"

"Mr. Sterling is a very busy man." She spreads her hands, palms up, like little wings. "I'm afraid I can't help you."

Jerry looks powerfully, coldly, into her sharp, beady eyes. He looks right through her, as if he can see her secret thoughts laid bare. And in his mind, he says the magic word. "Are you sure?"

"Of course I'm—Ooh! What's happening to the room? It's all spinning and shaky!" She clamps her hands onto the desk, like it's wildly swooping through space. "What did you say, sir?"

Jerry smiles confidently. "I need to see Mr. Sterling. It's important!"

The vulture lady is settling down a bit now, her claws still gripping the desk. "Well, I do have the authority to make exceptions, in very special cases. Please follow me, sir. Mr. Sterling's office is right this way."

She leads Jerry down a long hall lined with potted plants. They take an elevator up to the top floor. Another hallway. The carpet is soft and spongy. They bounce their way to a fancy door with a polished brass rectangle:

> MR. STERLING
> PRESIDENT

The lady knocks two times below the gleaming nameplate. After a brief pause, she knocks twice more.

"Yes, Matilda?"

"Someone very important to see you, sir. About an important matter."

"I'm busy. Who is this very important person?"

The vulture lady looks down helplessly at Jerry. "Jared J. Shore," he whispers. "And it's urgent!"

"Mr. Jared J. Shore, sir. And it's urgent!"

Jerry hears a clunk and shuffling feet. Then a clinking like a glass being set down. "Well, show him in then."

As they enter, Jerry sees a handsome man sitting behind a huge, polished desk. He has short, silver hair. He looks like a statue come to life. To one side, a putter leans against a chair. An empty drinking glass sits on a table beside it, and a golf ball in an ashtray.

The man's silver eyebrows shoot upwards. "Matilda! Is this some sort of joke? I was very busy."

"Sorry, sir." The lady squirms and rubs her head. "I don't know what came over me."

Jerry walks boldly up to the desk. "Sir, I'm the one who stopped the men from robbing your bank. Three years ago. I'd like a reward."

The handsome man makes a handsome laugh. "And what have you been doing for the past three years? Scheming up ways to suck money out of me?" He stands up very tall. "Will you leave immediately, or must I call security, young man?" The words "young man" slide out like a scornful sneer.

Jerry had planned to use The Look, but for some

mysterious reason, he changes his mind. "I wasn't going to ask you for money, sir. But my mama lost her job. We're very poor now, so—"

"Oh?" Mr. Sterling makes a puffy snort. "And what does your lazy-bones father do? Lie around the house all day?"

Without realizing it, Jerry clenches his fists. "My papa was killed in the War, sir. When I was five." A tear pops out onto his cheek.

As if by magic, Mr. Sterling's face totally changes. "I'm sorry, son. My younger brother was killed, too. By a hand grenade. In the dark."

Jerry stares into space. "My papa was shot in the back . . . because he was so far ahead of the others. Shot by one of our own soldiers. His best buddy told my mama after the War. He said my papa was too brave for his own good." A big tear slides down Jerry's trembling jaw.

The vulture lady gasps.

"There, there, my boy. Don't cry. I understand. War is a terrible, terrible thing." Mr. Sterling swallows hard. "What's your name again?"

"Jerry, sir. Jerry Shore."

"Well, Jerry. So you and your mother need money now?"

"Uh, yes, sir. We mostly have oatmeal for supper. And my mama . . . she doesn't eat much . . . so that I . . ."

The lady's hand flies to her mouth.

Mr. Sterling puts his arm around Jerry. "Well, I'm grateful for your help, my boy. You saved us a lot of money. How would you like a reward of ten thousand dollars?"

Jerry's mouth drops open. "Oh, yes, sir. Thank you, sir! My mama could pay all our bills . . . and have some money left over!"

"All right, then." Mr. Sterling smiles, pulling out his wallet. "Here's fifty bucks for now." He turns to the lady. "Matilda, write Mr. Shore a check for ten thousand dollars from the special fund."

"Yes, sir. Right away, sir!" She turns to Jerry. "Come with me, please, Mr. Shore."

"Get his address and phone number too. I want to keep track of this brave hero."

NINETEEN

JERRY'S mama squeals and hugs him so hard, he almost loses the strawberry sodas he guzzled on the way home.

Soon she pays off all her bills, and has plenty of money left.

School starts again, and Jerry is a hero. Treating his friends to ice cream doesn't hurt his popularity at all! Plus, he gratefully pays back the rest of the money he took for the magical objects. Only one person turns the money down.

Suzie Steele refuses to believe that her rusty-nail good-luck charm isn't real. She still wears it proudly on a loop of string around her neck. She even secretly holds her hand over the charm when teachers pass out test questions. She almost always knows the answers, too!

Jerry has lots of friends now, but he's still loyal to Monty Flowers. He remembers how Monty saved his butt! He plans to help Monty if he ever gets bullied by the other guys.

One day at lunch, Monty tells Jerry about his grandmother, who recently died. She looked a little like a stork, he says. Without thinking, he sketches a bird-like face on his paper napkin.

Jerry stares, wide-eyed. "Hey, Monty! I didn't know you could draw. That's really good!"

Monty slides a hand across the napkin. "That'th nothing." His face is red.

"No, it's good! Lemme see." He pulls Monty's hand away. "You've got talent! I wish I could draw like that. Aren't you glad you can?"

Monty hides a shy smile. "Yeth."

Jerry studies the sketch from different angles. "You got any more?"

"No," Monty says a little too quickly. "No more at all."

"You must! C'mon. Show me. *Please.*"

Monty hesitates. "All right. Come over to my houth tomorrow. But promith you won't tell anybody."

Jerry shrugs. "Sure, I promise. But I don't see—"

"You'll see why," says Monty, "when you see them."

*　　*　　*

Monty's house is even shabbier than Jerry's. His family must be really poor! The instant Jerry knocks, Monty opens the door, like he was waiting just inside it.

91

"Hi, Jerry. Look, I don't think I'd better—"

"Monty, I promised never to tell anybody about your drawings. We're friends. You've got to show me!"

Monty studies the floor. Then he looks carefully into Jerry's earnest, insisting eyes. "All right. But remember your promith!"

Up in his room, Monty pulls a big, worn folder from a shelf above his desk. "Here they are."

Jerry opens it up . . . and bursts out laughing. He laughs so hard, he almost drops the folder.

The first sketch shows Cromer Borkin, snorting through his nose. It looks like a cartoon drawing of a bull, but almost miraculously, it looks *exactly* like Cromer!

"Wow!" whistles Jerry. "That's amazing!"

"Don't tell," whispers Monty. "If Cromer finds out, he'll kill me!"

"Don't worry," says Jerry, eagerly flipping the page.

The next sketch shows a snooty-looking rat dressed like a schoolboy. But it's also Peter Wardly! Jerry laughs even louder. "How do you do it?" he asks.

"Maybe that's enough." Monty reaches for the folder. His face is shaky and gray.

Jerry dances away, turning his back. He's got to see more!

Soon he's laughed his way through about a dozen kids and several teachers. There's even a sketch of Monty himself, looking like a frightened little mouse. "You're a real artist, Monty! Who taught you?"

Monty looks down. "Nobody. I just . . . started drawing one day. I wish I could get lessons, but my dad says we can't afford it.

Jerry thinks for a while. "I know what we can do," he declares. "But you've got to let me show somebody the drawing of yourself. That way, none of the people you drew will get mad."

"Well . . . I geth that would be okay."

Jerry smiles. "Thanks, Monty."

Jerry doesn't say so, but he's got an ace in the hole. A powerful weapon in reserve. Maybe he won't need to use it, though. He persuaded Mr. Sterling without using The Look, didn't he?

*　　*　　*

The next day, during recess, Mrs. Meer looks up from her desk to see two boys standing there. She's the art teacher for the older students, who secretly call her "Mrs. Smear." There are rumors that she grease-paints her face.

"What do you want?" she asks, raising her black, shiny eyebrows. "Why didn't you knock?"

"I'm Jerry Shore," says Jerry. "And this is Monty Flowers. We're here to offer you a rare opportunity."

"An oppor— is this some kind of joke?"

"No," says Jerry. "Not at all. Take a look at this." He holds out Monty's picture of himself as a frightened little mouse. Standing beside him, Monty holds his breath.

Sniffing doubtfully, Mrs. Meer scans the drawing. "My!" She gasps. "This is truly remarkable. Amazing, in fact. Who drew this?"

"My friend Monty here," says Jerry. "Monty Flowers. See how much it looks like him?"

"I do indeed." Mrs. Meer smiles. "Just like a mouse, too! It's a bit rough, but it shows exceptional talent. Did you really do this, Monty?"

"Yeth." Monty looks down at the floor. "With the help of a mirror."

"Well, that's fair." Mrs. Meer laughs. "Who's your drawing teacher?"

"He doesn't have one," Jerry blurts. "His parents can't afford it. But here's the opportunity I mentioned. If you give Monty free art lessons, once a week, at your house, he'll give you ten percent of all the money he makes when he becomes a famous artist. How's that for a bargain?"

Mrs. Meer smiles. "Well, he does have remarkable talent . . ."

"He certainly does!" Jerry exclaims. "He's a future Rembrandt."

"Jerry!" Monty grabs his arm. "Maybe you'd better not . . ."

Jerry looks deeply into his eyes. "Monty, this will be good for both of you. You'll see."

"All right," says Mrs. Meer. "It's a deal."

Once again, Jerry feels good that he didn't need to use the power of The Look. Could it be because . . . he's getting help from his Higher Self? "I'll keep trying not to use The Look," he thinks. "Unless it's really an emergency."

Little does he know what a desperate emergency is soon to rear its head! But you'll have to wait for the next book, *Jerry's Madness,* to read about that.

Acknowledgments

I am deeply grateful to Jeff Cox and Sam Cohen for their numerous helpful suggestions. Also to Paul Cash, for his crucial insights. Anything the reader finds objectionable is not their fault, but mine.